IF SNOW FALLS

A STORY FOR DECEMBER BY

JON AGEE

A SUNBURST BOOK
FARRAR, STRAUS AND GIROUX

To my grandmother, Sallie Murphy

Copyright © 1982 by Jon Agee
All rights reserved
First published by Pantheon Books, 1982
Library of Congress catalog card number: 96-2299
Published in Canada by HarperCollins*Canada*Ltd
Printed in the United States of America
Sunburst edition, 1996
Second printing, 1996

If snow falls

when it's windy

while it's colder

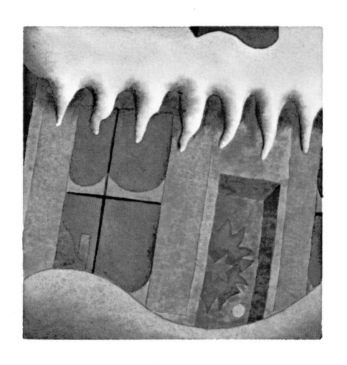

and colder

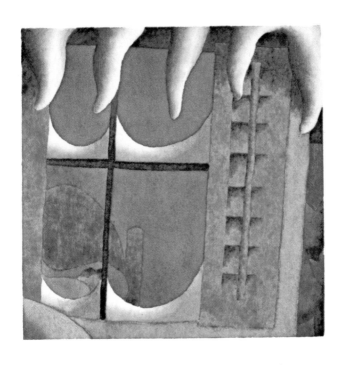

and nobody has stepped

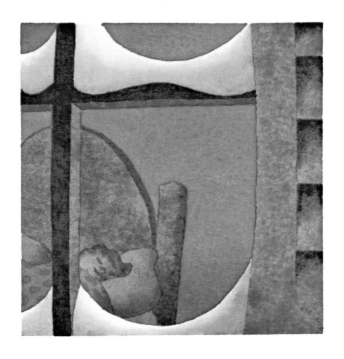

in the snow yet

I will dream

of an old man

like my grandpa

who dances a jig

stretches

and arrives

at a workshop

with pots, paints

and parrots watching

as he works

so quietly

on a secret

he puts in a sack.

Then with it

he'll go

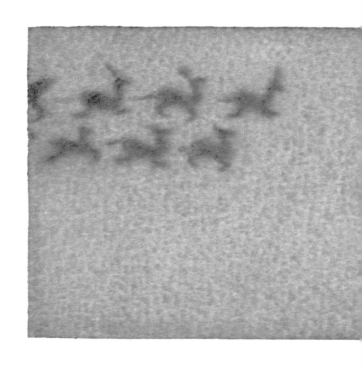

across snow

nobody has stepped in

while it's colder

and colder

when it's windy

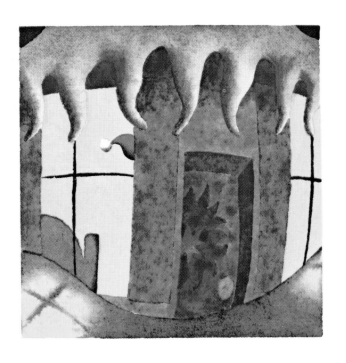

if snow falls…